E
FICTION
MACE

Jill McElmurry

Mess Pets

SeaStar Books ❖ New York

Hannah and Hilary shared a room.
They had different ways of doing things
and different points of view
about this and that and what goes where
like popcorn, pajamas, underwear,
and empty soda cans.

"Hannah, Hannah, garbage canna,
    fell in love with a rotten banana!
When we asked her, 'How's it smell?'
    she said, 'I like it very well!'"

sang Hilary.

But Hannah liked her cozy nest
and way down deep inside the mess
between pizza crusts and grubby socks
something started to grow,

and grow

and grow

and grow

and grow

until it came out to say hello.

"I'll call you Mr. Peel," she said,
"for the fruit stuck in your hair."

They had great fun paw-painting.

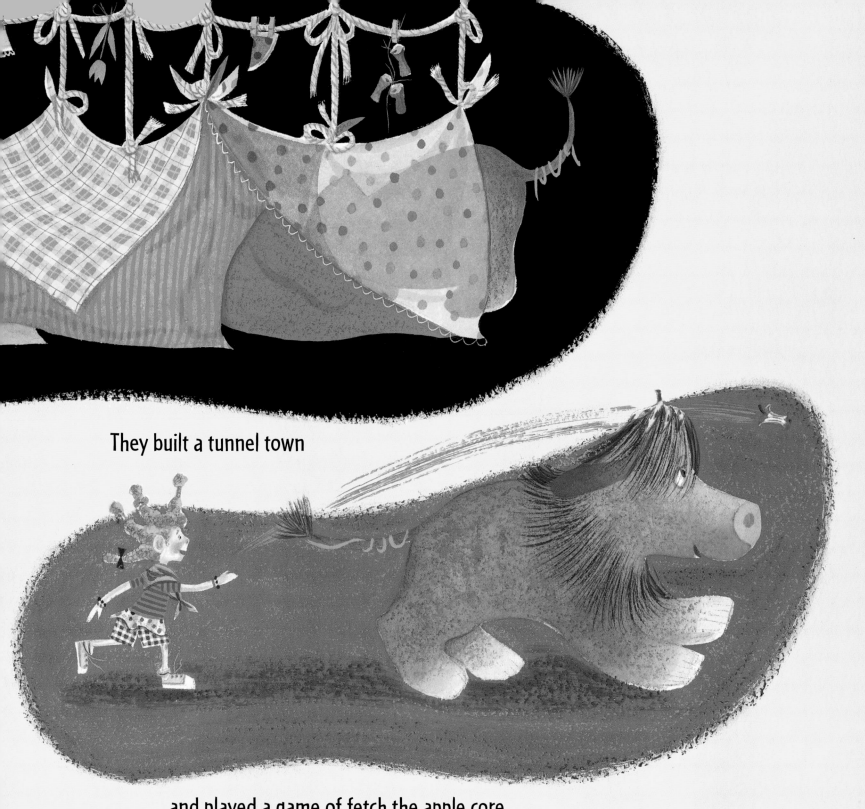

They built a tunnel town

and played a game of fetch the apple core.

Hilary stole some of Hannah's mess
and chanted a secret chant,
"Oh, Master of messes,
and jelly-stained dresses,
oh, sticky puddles of goo,
oh, dust bunnies, mud pies, and mushy bananas,
make me a pet much better than Hannah's!"

Hilary named her pet Tip Top.
"What a tip-top pet!" she said.

"She can use a computer,

do tricks on her scooter,

and whip up a batch of ice cream!"

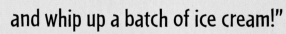

"HA!" replied Hannah,
"Mr. Peel is the best!
He does modern ballet
in his own special way
and sings as he makes chocolate syrup."

"Come on," Hannah said,

and they leaped headfirst into the mess.

TO HANNAH'S PLACE

STRING SHRUB

TREE OF MUDDY DRESSES

GUACAMOLE PLANT

PINK FROSTING DEPOT

"Welcome, my friends!" called a creature named Jinx.
"Where are we?" asked Hilary nervously.
"This is where messes begin," said Jinx,
"and where all messes return.
Trashy messes, splashy messes,
messy rooms and muddy dresses,
blotchy blobs of messiness,
and tangled balls of string.
Waxy ears and dirty faces,
horrid heaps in hard-to-reach places,
gooey gobs of who-knows-what,
and other messy things.

"In Mess World," said Jinx, "Hannah is a star."

"Mr. Peel ran away!" whined Hannah.
"And Tip Top too!" wailed Hilary.
"Last I heard," said Jinx,
"they were headed toward Gum Wad Hill."
"Oh no!" Hannah cried,
"We'll never get past the cliffs of Old Shoes Canyon."

"With my dustpan and broom,
we'll get there tonight!"
said Hilary, leading the way . . .

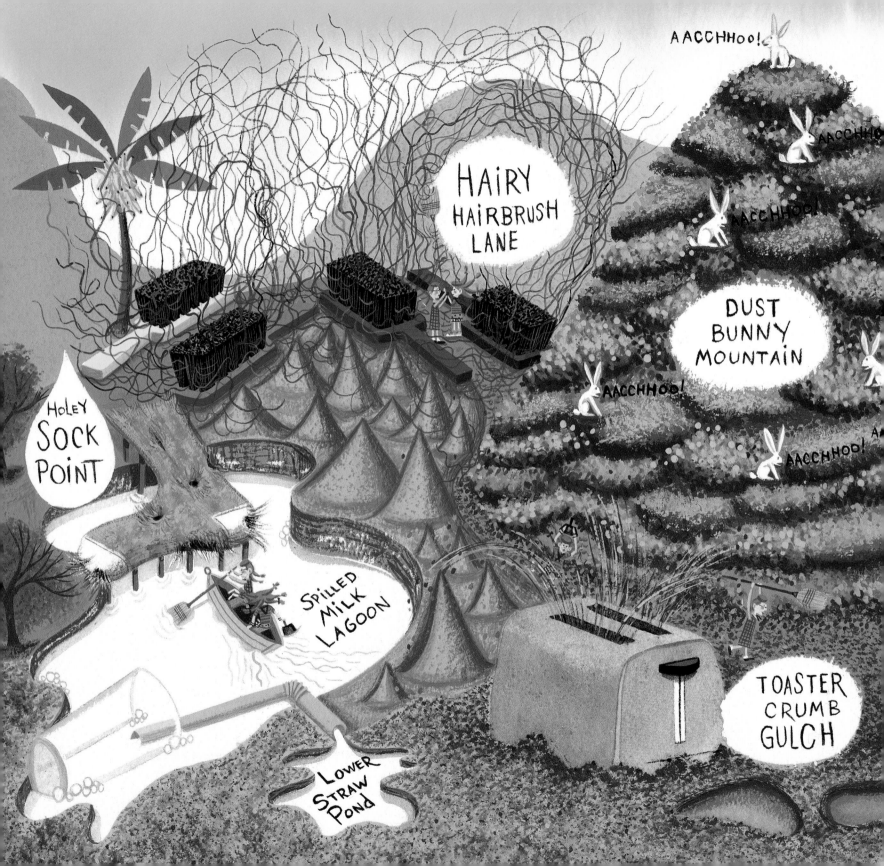

OLD
SHOES
CANYON

PUDDLES
of
GOO

over Spilled Milk Lagoon
to Holey Sock Point,
down Hairy Hairbrush Lane,
past Dust Bunny Mountain,
through Toaster Crumb Gulch,
to Puddles of Goo
(where they stopped for some lunch).
The cliffs of Old Shoes Canyon
they crossed with the help of a broom,
and found Mr. Peel and Tip Top
saying things that they'd heard . . .

Your chocolate
has lumps!

"There's no need to fight!" said Hilary.
"A dash of fur and a couple of lumps
won't hurt a bit
when we mix them up . . .

in a giant banana split!"

Then the round-tummied pets
curled up for a snooze
as Hilary and Hannah put on their shoes...

and went home for a little less mess.

For Eric, with whom I share my room.

SEASTAR BOOKS
A division of NORTH-SOUTH BOOKS INC.

First published in the United States by SeaStar Books, a division of North-South Books Inc., New York.
Published simultaneously in Canada by North-South Books, an imprint of Nord-Süd Verlag AG, Gossau Zürich, Switzerland.

Library of Congress Cataloging-in-Publication Data is available.
The artwork for this book was prepared by using gouache.
Book design by Nicole de las Heras

ISBN 1-58717-174-0 (trade edition)
1 3 5 7 9 HC 10 8 6 4 2
ISBN 1-58717-175-9 (library edition)
1 3 5 7 9 LE 10 8 6 4 2

Printed in Malaysia

For more information about our books, and the authors and artists who create them, visit our web site: **www.northsouth.com**

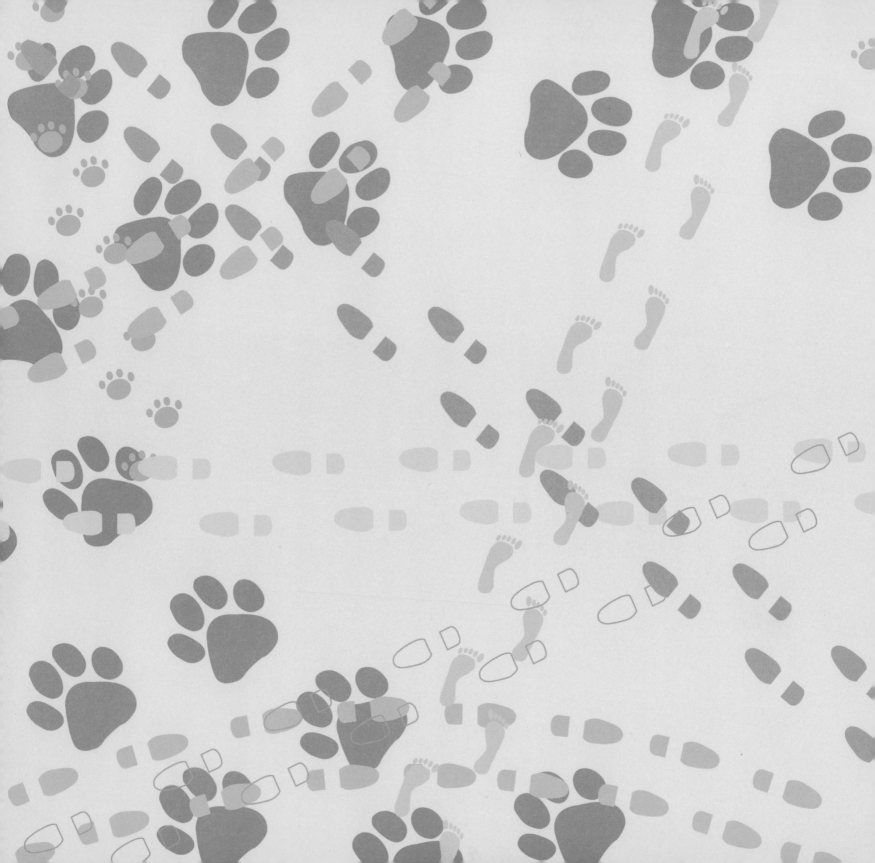